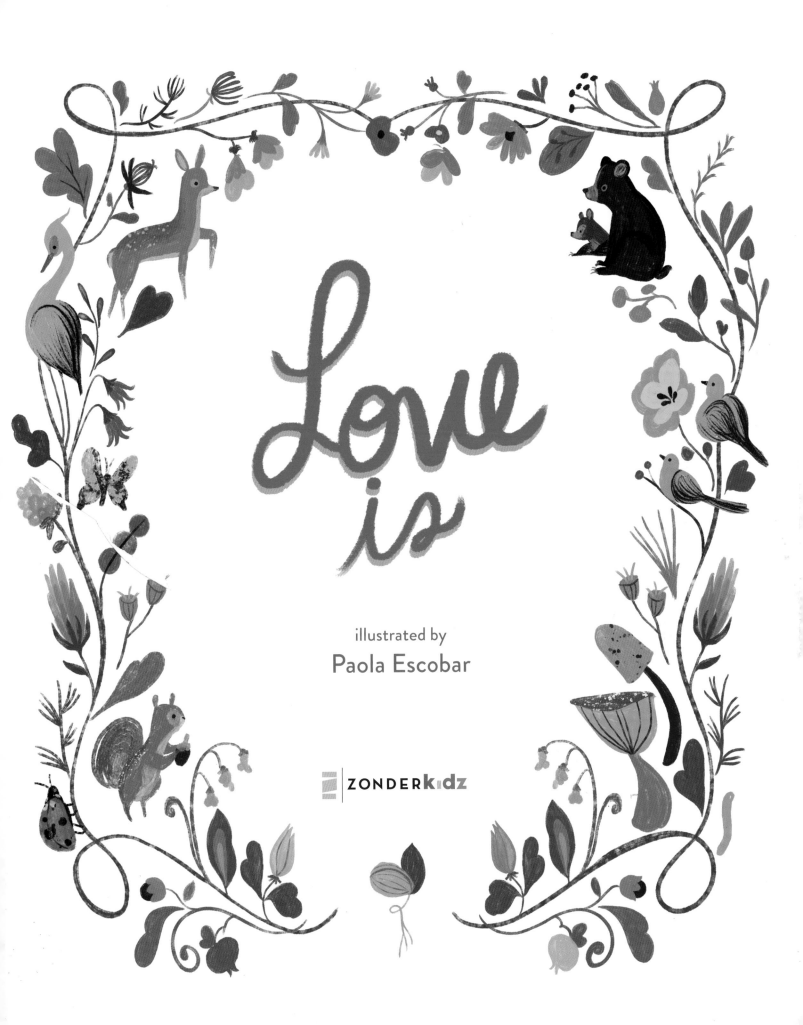

Love is

illustrated by
Paola Escobar

ZONDERkidz

Love is patient.

Love is kind.

Love does not want

what belongs to others.

It does not brag.

other people.

It does not look out

for its own interests.

It does not easily

become angry.

It does not keep track

of other people's wrongs.

Love is not happy with evil.

But it is full of joy when

the truth is spoken.

It always protects.

It always trusts.

It always hopes.

It never gives up.

Love never fails.